THE WORLD OF CHINESE MAGAZINE
《汉语世界》杂志社编

CHINA IN SCOPE

镜像中国

SINCE1897 The Commercial Press

2011, Beijing

Publisher: Yu Dianli

Production Supervisor: Zhou Hongbo

Mastermind / Chief Editor: Cao Quan

Art director / Designer: Yuke Wang

Executive Editors: Wen Xuechun, He Hongtao, Zhao Lei

Proofreaders: Yu Libin, Zhao Yuhong

Special thanks to:

Zhu Xiaojian, H.R.Lan (USA), David N. Tool (USA), Li Bing,
Cui Yonghua, Andy Deemer (USA), Jonathan Heeter (USA),
Robert Lewis Livingston (USA), Nicholas Richards (Canada),
Tian Wenzhu, Zhao Zhankun

CHAPTERS

GOING HOME

Huíjiā

回家

Theme by Ashwen
Article by Echo
Photographs by Hao Guanhai
Translated by Liu Lu

March 2007, Longyan, Fujian Province. Children are going home along an ancient street.

February 2007, Nanjing, Jiangsu Province. People with big and small bags are often seen in cities. Maybe they are going home after a business trip, after traveling, or they are students coming back for the holidays to visit parents they have not seen for a long time. When tired, everyone longs to get back to his or her own sweet home.

July 2007, Beijing. To those who work in a city, the routine of going to work, buying groceries, going home, and cooking repeats itself in a simple but comfortable way.

July 2006, Kaili, Guizhou Province. A father is going home with wedding gifts from the groom's family followed by his daughter who got married earlier in the year. According to the tradition of the Miao village of Basha, Congjiang Dong and Miao Autonomous County, in southeast Guizhou Province, on June 15 of the lunar calendar, a bride should go back to her parents' to celebrate the "New Rice Tasting Festival."

February, 2007, Liaocheng, Shandong Province. On the second day of the Chinese New Year, according to local tradition, this wife, with her husband and children, is going home happily down a county road to visit her parents and bring them gifts.

September 2007, Altay, Xinjiang. Herdsmen in Xinjiang are "going home" on camelback from their summer home in the high mountain pastures to their winter home in the low land pastures. Their "mobile homes" on the backs of the camels accompany them everywhere.

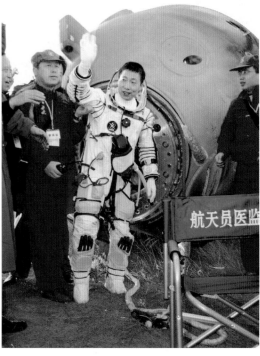

April 2006, Xichang, Sichuan Province. Three farmers on their way home, each with a full load. The silence on the road is like their life, wordless but indicative of strength and great perseverance.

On the morning of Oct. 16, 2003, the first Chinese astronaut, Yang Liwei, steps out of the module of Shenzhou No.5 manned spaceship which just returned from outer space in Ulan Qab, Inner Mongolia. After circling the earth 14 times, he finally steps onto the earth again and will soon be going home.

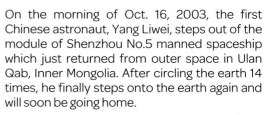

January 2007, Beijing. During the Spring Festival, workers return home to the countryside with their plastic-wrapped belongings. After a year's hard work, they can relax for a while with their families at home.

CITYEXPRESSIONS

Chéngshì Biǎoqíng

城市表情

By Echo

Photographs by Alexander Berg

A city is like a huge stage on which everyone will be touched deeply by a story, a memory, or just a moment. The photographer Alexander Berg, fascinated by such special moments, came to create a portrait of Beijing. Thanks for his contribution so that we are now granted with an opportunity to explore the city and its people. All the images herein are courtesy of Alexander Berg.

I have taken over 370 photos here in Beijing, and fallen in love with different faces on different days, in different moods. – Alexander Berg

Each city has its own expression.

I was surprised by how much joy I felt in the people here in Beijing, and how open people were. There is an honesty that is so available here. – Alexander Berg

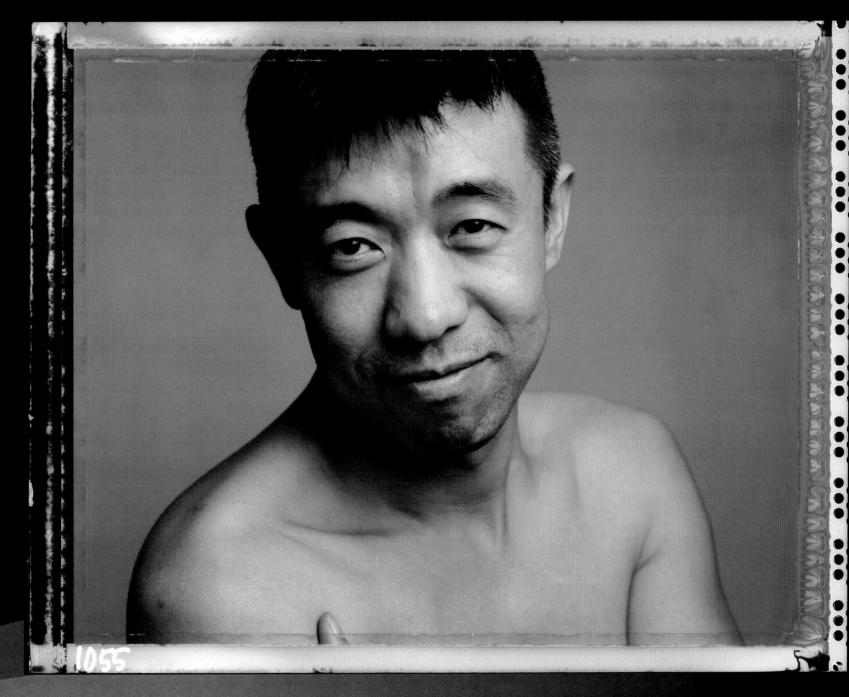

1055

It feels both ancient and futuristic in Beijing, all at once. Amazing and immense. – Alexander Berg

Alexander Berg:
Originally from Stockholm, Sweden, Alexander Berg has been photographing for about 20 years. He studied, and now also teaches, at Parson's School of Design. He lives and works in New York City, and his solo exhibitions there include One Shot and Nippon. Group shows in New York City include Moments of Clarity and Celebrities. His portraiture can also be seen in Planet Magazine, Manhattan File, etc. He has also photographed an ashtanga yoga book published in Sweden, Finland and France. We went to visit him in the Beijing gallery and raised some questions.

fànguǎn
饭馆
RESTAURANT

Whose eyes are peering from behind the glass wall?

WINDOW
VIEWS

Chuāng • Jǐng
窗 • 景

Theme by Ashwen
Article by Echo
Photographs by Liu Jianfeng

kuàicāndiàn
快餐店
FAST-FOOD RESTAURANT

People become quieter as the night deepens. Romance fills the cool summer air.

shìpǐndiàn
饰品店
ORNAMENT STORE

It's a world of splendid colors. Wherever your gaze wanders, it's a bright, glistening picture of the multi-colored life of youth.

bàokāntíng
报刊亭
NEWSPAPER STAND

Several decades have passed; the newspaper stand is still here. Not jealous of those tall buildings behind, not in pursuit of a glamorous appearance; it is happy to simply be warm company to those returning home at night.

fúzhuāng jiāgōngdiàn
服装加工店
TAILOR'S SHOP

The old tailor's shop has changed greatly, with new modern signs and images on its windows. Only the reflections of the old trees on them make us wonder: where has the old bespectacled tailor gone?

kāfēiguǎn
咖啡馆
CAFE

Outside the window, the new CCTV building is rising from the ground, while the small cafe is as quiet as ever.

jiǔbā
酒吧
BAR

A reunion between a teacher and her young student at a bar. With its red, checkered tablecloth, a puppet in a Qing dress to one side, and the watchtower of the Forbidden City as the background, the cozy little bar is the perfect place for a pleasant *deja vu* conversation.

jiàoshì
教室
CLASSROOM

It is a holiday but all the kids are studying attentively in the classroom – all except one naughty boy who keeps looking out the window. Perhaps, his heart has leaped over the windowsill into nature where the sun shines and flowers bloom.

lùbiān xiǎochītān
路边小吃摊
STREET STAND

Three people are having breakfast at one table, silent but totally at ease with each other. It is a common scene on the morning street – strangers becoming acquaintances once seated around a breakfast table.

Hòuhǎi Gōngyuán
后海公园
HOUHAI PARK

We live in a big world with many dazzling scenes around us. Why not capture the most beautiful and frame them?

A DISPLAY OF OLYMPIC TREASURES

Àoyùn Bǎobèi Xiù

奥运宝贝秀

Model: Hu Chen
Photographs by Zhu Jiang
Translated by Xie Shijian

Àoyùn Bǎobèi Chuānshàng Shēn

奥运宝贝穿上身

The Outfit of an Olympic Cheerleader
Including Olympic T-shirt, tie, miniskirt, bag, water bottle, purse, artificial umbrella, and glasses.

Niǎocháo Dìyī Pǐn Gāngdiāo
鸟巢第一榀钢雕
Steel Sculpture
of the First Truss of the Bird's Nest
The sculpture is made of the steel saved after canceling the movable roof of the Bird's Nest. It is strictly modeled after the first truss of the National Stadium with a ratio of 1:100, with the pattern and length of every steel bar in accordance with that of the actual.

Àoyùn Qìnggōng Jué
奥运庆功爵
Olympic Goblet for Celebration
Jue (three-legged goblet) is an ancient Chinese wine vessel. The implication of the Olympic goblet is to celebrate the success of the Games. The goblet itself and its base are made of gold-plated alloy, with the Olympic emblem in relief, the Games logo, patterns of clouds and ripples.

Gāngdiāo Huǒjù
钢雕火炬
Steel Sculpture of Olympic Torch

Dùjīn "Niǎocháo"
镀金 "鸟巢"
Gilded National Stadium "The Bird's Nest"

Liúlí "Shuǐlìfāng"
琉璃 "水立方"
Colored Glaze National Aquatic Center "The Water Cube"

Qiānzújīn Àoyùn Bǎoxǐ

千足金奥运宝玺

24k Gold Olympic Seal

Yù Fúwá

玉福娃

Jade Olympic Mascot "Fuwa"

Táocí Huāpíng

陶瓷花瓶

China Vase

THE KINGDOM OF BICYCLES

Zìxíngchē Wángguó

自行车王国

Theme by Tian Yan, Ashwen
Article by Echo
Photographs by Ashwen, Echo, Chen Han, Chen You
Translated by Chen Liping

guǎnggào
广告
Chángchūn
长春

The bicycle ad team, which has come into existence in recent years, is a unique scene along the street.

shàngbān
上班
Zhèngzhōu
郑州

Cyclists and motorists in the morning rush hour.

xiūchē
修车
Běijīng
北京

In July 2007, a repairer, a bicycle and a folding stool are all the components for a bicycle repair stand, a place many cyclists eagerly seek.

sānrénxíng
三人行
Qínhuángdǎo
秦皇岛

Three-rider bicycles are very popular in this beach city.

zhìzào
制造
Tiānjīn
天津

China is the "Kingdom of Bicycles." Statistics show that China's annual output of bicycles totaled 85,000,000 in 2006. With a complete production system established, its output and export account for more than 60% of the world's total.

yùn mùcái
运木材
Yákèshí
牙克石

In November 2006, a couple load their bicycle with wood. In northern China, the bicycle serves as an important transport vehicle. Of course, it's a real test of riding skills to cycle along a precipitous and curving mountain path, especially when the bicycle is heavily loaded.

liúyǐng
留影
Lánzhōu
兰州

In the winter of 1957, three young doctors smile shyly in the picture. When they graduated from the university, bicycles were enviable luxuries for them.

chuānyuè gāoyuán
穿越高原
Yǎ'ān
雅安

In June, 2006, a cyclist rides alone on a snow-covered plateau. Many prefer a biking tour nowadays, pedaling their way through nature.

jià qǔ
嫁娶
Tāizhōu
台州

In October 2004, the bridegroom takes his bride home by bicycle, saving money but lending interest to the wedding.

gǎnjí
赶集
Bǎojī
宝鸡

On a snowy country road, a businessman carries as many lanterns as possible to the fair.

qíshǒu
骑手
Běijīng
北京

In June 2007, a little cyclist rides with pride.

shàngxué
上学
Línyí
临沂

In December 2005, a mother takes her child to school, braving the wind and snow. The jumbled ruts in the snow are indelible in the childhood memory.

zài yǔ zhōng
在雨中
Wǔhàn
武汉

Cyclists in raincoats of various colors. Most Chinese cities have lanes exclusively for bicycles.

xué Xījù
学锡剧
Wúxī
无锡

In May 2007 inside Wuxi Opera Museum, Jiangsu Province, an overseas visitor, with a prop in hand, is "rehearsing" with a Wuxi Opera singer. Foreign residents in Wuxi take this opportunity to experience the charm of Wuxi Opera.

ON THE
ROAD

Rén Zài Lùshang
人在路上

Theme by Sun Liang
Article by Meng Hua
Photographs by A Chun
Translated by Peng Yu

dǎgōng
打工
Fúzhōu
福州

In May 2007 in Fuzhou, Fujian Province, Benjamin Ross from the U.S.A. works in a local barber's shop. By working there 10 hours a day and 6 days a week for a month and earning a monthly wage of no more than 1,000 yuan, he experienced the life of an ordinary Chinese worker.

jiāo Yīngyǔ
教英语
Chángzhì
长治

In September 2006 Changzhi, Shanxi Province, South African Carl teaches English by playing games with the teachers and children at the Yizhi Kindergarten.

yuèdú
阅读
Běijīng
北京

In July 2007, an overseas student stops to read. The Chinese character on the T-shirt is 拆 "demolish" – a word often seen on Chinese streets. Buildings to be demolished are often painted with this character.

huányóu Zhōngguó
环游中国
Liányúngǎng
连云港

In April 2007, a tour-of-China motorcade of 15 vintage cars from abroad drives through the city of Lianyungang, Jiangsu Province. The motorcade set off from Hong Kong, and the theme of this event was to "Commemorate the 10th Anniversary of the Handover of Hong Kong to China."

chuántǒng hūnlǐ
传统婚礼
Jǐnán
济南

In August 2005 in the scenic area of Daming Lake, Jinan, Shandong Province, Jan – a young Dutch man and a Jinan girl held a traditional Chinese wedding. At the ceremony, the new couple went through the ritual of taking a sedan chair, uncovering the bride's red headkerchief and bowing to each other.

xué zuò Zhōngguócài
学做中国菜
Nánjīng
南京

In Nanjing, Jiangsu Province, a Yemeni student is learning Chinese cooking in his Chinese friend's home. Far away from home, foreigners take such opportunities not only to learn about Chinese cuisine but also to feel the closeness and the warmth of Chinese families.

wèi chǒngwù zuò "xīnlǐ zhìliáo"
为宠物做 "心理治疗"
Wúxī
无锡

dào "huángjīndì" gōngzuò
到 "黄金地" 工作
Shànghǎi
上海

zhǔfù shēnghuó
主妇生活
Běijīng
北京

In July 2007, a foreign housewife is contemplating clothes for her child.

In April 2007 at a pet hospital in Wuxi, Jiangsu, Sara and a pet dog are "communicating intimately." Sara is a volunteer assigned by the Association of Veterinarians of Small Animals in the U.S.A. to work in Wuxi on a China-US exchange program for pet protection.

More and more people from overseas are coming to Shanghai to hunt for jobs. At present, there are hundreds of thousands of foreigners working in Shanghai. Marco Polo referred to Shanghai as "a land of gold," and it remains so.

ART AND SOUL

Yìshù   Zài Zhōngguó
艺术在中国

By Sun Liang
Photographs by PHOTOTIME, Tian Li, Meng Hua, A Chun
Translated by Sun Liang

píyǐngxì
皮影戏
Zhèjiāng
浙江

August, 2005, Haining, Zhejiang. An old master of piying (Chinese shadow puppet) performing his art with concentrated attention. Piying created a sensation in Europe when first introduced in the 17th century.

wǔ lóngdēng
舞龙灯
Sìchuān
四川

October 2006. Ya'an, Sichuan. A team of dragon dancers in the street. Women have always been among the most imaginative, inspired, and powerful inventors and preservers of local heritage.

píyǐng
皮影
Sìchuān
四川

June 2005, Jinli Street, Chengdu. Exquisite *piying* (Chinese shadow puppets) attracting passers-by. Chinese communities continue to rediscover their own artistic heritage as outsiders bring in fresh perspectives.

cǎihuì bīngmǎyǒng
彩绘兵马俑
Shǎnxī
陕西

Xi'an, October 2006. Local artists responded enthusiastically when the government of Xi'an, the celebrated capital of the Tang Dynasty, invited them to "modernize" copies of the celebrated terra-cotta soldiers.

jiǎnzhǐ
剪纸
Shǎnxī
陕西

Shaanxi, February 2007. Paper-cuts stall in front of the old Guanzhong Imperial Academy in Xi'an, capital of the Tang Dynasty in ancient China. Commerce and tourism revived local art and artisanship. Note the range of the artwork: from traditional zodiac animals to a silhouette of Mao.

piàoyǒu chàng Jīngjù
票友唱京剧
Shāndōng
山东

Jinan, April 2007. An amateur Peking Opera troupe perfecting their art in one of the city's public parks. Art around the world has been a most powerful form of social fabric.

èrrénzhuàn
二人转
Liáoníng
辽宁

April 2006, Liaoyang, Liaoning. An old couple set youthful passion flowing as a star-performance duo in a park. The expanding ranks of aging citizens provide an invaluable artistic repertoire.

jiētóu huàjiā
街头画家
Guǎngxī
广西

July 2005, Yangshuo County, Guangxi. The street artists drawing quick sketches for several foreign tourists. Like their comrades from Manhattan to the Riviera, the intrepid group strives for mastery through thick and thin.

mùhòu
幕后
Shānxī
山西

September 2005, Linfen, Shanxi. Temple fairs are a folk tradition in the villages of north China, where the folk art is a popular form of performance.

↑
Yuánxiāo Jié dàxì
元宵节大戏
Zhèjiāng
浙江

February 2006. A county opera called "Wuxi Opera" at the Lantern Festival. Private and community-sponsored theater in rural China today pays tribute to the very essence of art: as a ritual, a celebration of public space, a confirmation of community values and private aspirations played out in the vast theater of life beyond this little make-up stage.

huàjù
话剧
Běijīng
北京
↓

The first modern drama in Chinese, Uncle Tom's Cabin, came into existence in China 100 years ago. Built in 1954, the first professional theater in Beijing, the Capital Theater for modern drama performance, has witnessed the ebb and flow of modern drama in new China.

huàláng
画廊
Běijīng
北京

April 2005, the 798 Art Zone, Beijing. In the new galleries and studios now occupying the enormous facilities of former, state-owned factories, young art students can see faded slogans painted next to huge pieces of abstract art.

wǔdǎo
舞蹈
Guìzhōu
贵州

nóngjiālè
农家乐
Liáoníng
辽宁

Guizhou, August 2005. A dancer from Tunbao, where local forms of worship adopted elements of Confucianism, Taoism, and Buddhism to create a unique form of dance theater, is captured in a moment of pride and joy with a digital camera. For an ordinary art lover, the technological revolution opens up intriguing possibilities to record and share art as it is lived.

February 2007, Zhuanghe County, Liaoning. A happy party of villagers in the mountain area. Art can be seen everywhere. The melody played by different musical instruments is something we call "life."

CHINA AT PLAY

Zhōngguó Wánshuǎ

中国玩耍

By Sun Liang
Photographs by Zhao Bingzhong, Zhu Jiang, A Shi, Tian Li, Wang Zhiqiang, Sun Liang, Qin Dongxia, Jiang Fuxiang
Translated by Sun Liang

dǒu kōngzhú
抖空竹
Běijīng
北京

liùniǎo
遛鸟
Běijīng
北京

Beijing , September 2005. An old man "walking" his pet birds as kindergarten children flutter by. Will all ways of play pass down through time?

dìshū
地书
Běijīng
北京

November 2005. Beihai Park, Beijing. An amateur calligrapher writes a quote from a Tang poem, with a sponge-brush, in water fetched from what used to be the back lake of the Imperial Palace.

fàng fēngzheng
放风筝
Běijīng
北京

May 2005. Kites soar on a gusty morning in Beijing, in a sky crowded with skyscrapers.

wán bīnghuátī
玩冰滑梯
Hā'ěrbīn
哈尔滨

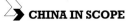

tiào píjīnr
跳皮筋儿
Shěnyáng
沈阳

Even in times of scarcity, generations of Chinese girls set off their first dreams with the chords of rubber bands.

tīqiú
踢球
Tiānjīn
天津

Tianjin, July 2006. The city's face is changing at dazzling speed as children, yet to embrace the promise and weight of the future, turn piles of rubble into playgrounds.

xiàqí
下棋
Běijīng
北京

November 2006. A game of chess in the heart of Beijing. Play was a part of socializing with neighbors of public life, before computer games made it possible to play in virtual intimacy.

tiàowǔ
跳舞
Běijīng
北京

September 2006, waltzing by the walls of the Forbidden City to music by Johann Strauss Jr. from a tape-recorder on the back of a bicycle. The middle-aged are the mainstay of the open-air ballroom-dancing movement across China.

chōu bīnghóur
抽冰猴儿
Hā'ěrbīn
哈尔滨

Taoran Ting Park, Beijing, and the outskirts of Harbin. Time honored yo-yo play rejuvenated among the young-at-heart. Children won't lose ways of play as long as adults refuse to forget about them.

wán bīngchē
玩冰车
Běijīng
北京

Winter, playing with ice in Harbin and Beijing. The way we play is closely associated to nature and its seasonal wonders.

wán gǎlāhā
玩嘎拉哈
Jílín
吉林

Winter, catching sheep's anklebones on a brick *kang* bed in northern China. The game is fading away in China's bigger cities.

tī jiànzi
踢毽子
Běijīng
北京

The power of play lies in its contagiousness across boundaries. A Korean tourist picked up the game intuitively.

ENJOYING
FITNESS
ACTIVITIES

Jiànshēn Lè Fān Tiān
健身乐翻天

By Echo
Photographs by Shi Tianyou

四川省成都市
CHENGDU, SICHUAN PROVINCE

Citizens from 10 communities in Chengdu compete in the Public Facilities Contest.

More and more people engage in fitness activities nowadays under a Nationwide Physical Fitness Program, established in 1995 by the State Physical Culture Administration, which aims to promote physical fitness nationwide. Public health facilities are popular in parks, squares, schoolyards, residential quarters and other convenient locations. They are enjoyed by people of all ages.

四川省广安市
GUANG' AN, SICHUAN PROVINCE

Farmers enjoy the exercise equipment in the park.

浙江省温岭市
WENLING, ZHEJIANG PROVINCE

Children cross the iron-chain bridge at the village's public fitness club where there are various types of body-building equipment.

北京
BEIJING

A mother and her son exercise in their community.

Upper right: Ready for the Sun—Liu Dan
Upper left: Don't smile for the camera— Sun Huijun
Lower left: Quiet on the inside—Peng Xuanzhi
Lower right: What-a-sucker—Suo Hao

Beijing Youth

STREET STYLE

Jiētóu Shíshàng
街头时尚

Article and Photographs by
Josh Haller

Walking through the streets of Beijing has changed in the recent past. More and more Chinese youth are showing off their artistic flare via clothing. Here's a glimpse at some authentic, raw Chinese style.

Posing at the gate - Lisa

Stepping out of the shadows - Yang Guang

Upper left: A couple for sore eyes—Li Changyin and Xia Zhen
Upper right: To the mall!!!
Lower left: New to town (Guangzhou) —Zhang Shining (Shelly) and Tim
Lower right: Friends for tables—left to right: Sun Huijun, Liu Dan, Wang Amao

Call waiting--Tata

Nervous smiles--Xiao Jie

WHERE DREAMS BEGIN

Red Star, a school for migrant workers' children

Mèng Kāishǐ de Dìfang
梦开始的地方

Article and Photographs by
Kobuta

Migrant workers form special communities. They build cities, they work for minimum wage and they are the base of the pyramid. In many migrant worker families, children grow up in the city their parents built, roaming with their families like nomads, from an early age.

I visited Red Star Primary School where there were shabby classrooms and dedicated teachers; however, the children looked just the same as any city children in public schools. They like games, they like school, they like making friends and making fun of each other. They smile. And all of them have vivid dreams about their future. It made me feel like I was doing something meaningful when I froze their images in these frames.

Not camera shy!

"In many migrant worker families, children grow up in the cities their parents built, roaming with their families like nomads, from an early age."

Can their parents read these performance reports?

Will the sound of hope resound from within this horn?

Children being taken home by their parents

Not enough new textbooks for everyone

Many children didn't turn up after the New Year; the teacher can do nothing about it.

"All of them have vivid dreams about their future."

THE ONGOING LIFE OF CLASSIC DRAMA

The pupils of traditional Chinese theater

Xìqǔ   Zhī Lù
戏曲之路

Article and Photographs by Asen

The place: Middle School Affiliated to the National Academy of Chinese Theatre Arts (NACTA), AKA "the cradle of Chinese theater performers." Its mission: to find the apt of the apt of China's young performers.

Every year, NACTA scours the country, far and wide, for potential students. Those gifted enough to be selected spend the next six years undergoing rigorous training in hopes of eventually entering into China's elite group of theater performers. Here is a glimpse into what the boys and girls of "the cradle" have to go through on a daily basis, in order to fulfill their potential and live out their dreams, mastering one of China's most ancient and revered art forms.

Life as a child and performer: a constant balancing act.

In its early stages, training revolves heavily around developing Chinese theater's core concepts of flexibility and balance.

Rehearsing for a big performance, the children take the time to learn an essential part of drama performing — makeup.

Waiting in the wings.

The girls exude charm as they give off an aura that is simultaneously lively and shy.

Due to its highly standardized nature, teachers of Chinese theater are to be as meticulous as possible. To this day they are known for busting out the age-old method of using a bamboo stick to measure the preciseness of each of their students' moves.

The school's 10-minute-between-class breaks are no different from those of other schools—that is, if you excuse the occasional acrobatic display.

Serious future performers or not, in the end, boys will be boys. These four have just discovered that their horseplay has resulted in runny makeup. Back to the dressing room.

Leg stretching. From head to toe, the children immerse themselves in their roles as future performers.

A respite — kid-style.

Young students backstage, watching as the path of their future becomes bright.

In a reading class. Children in those remote mountain areas are really thirst for knowledge, especially in popular sciences. The expression of a child absorbed in a book is truly unforgettable.

THOSE DAYS OF SUNSHINE

Nàxiē Yángguāng Cànlàn de Rìzi

那些阳光灿烂的日子

Theme by He Hongtao
Article by He Hongtao, Yue Yunlong
Photographs by Volunteer Team from
Hua Zhong Normal University
Translated by Nicholas Richards

From July 16th to 25th this summer our volunteer team from Hua Zhong Normal University went to work as volunteer teachers at Anjing Primary School in Xingjing County, Sichuan Province. Our task was to serve as counselors for the students, emotionally as well as academically. In the short span of ten days, we studied and lived together with the students and had a lot of fun together. Those were true days of sunshine.

During emotional guidance class, student Hu Xiaoling finished her self-portrait assignment. On her picture she wrote: "My home is in a forest on a fine spring day: I hope I'm as lovable as a bunny."

The school needs English teachers most of all. Currently, their English classes are all taught by teachers of Chinese, not surprisingly, the teaching is not very effective and students have little interest in learning. Therefore, we put most of our effort into teaching English. We tried to arouse the students' interest by encouraging each and every student to answer questions in English.

志勤学　文明守纪

We were really happy to see that, after a few counseling classes, students started to raise their hands, ask questions and give their opinions. Look, here you can really see the confidence on their faces.

After counseling classes, these young children finally overcame their timidity and started to dance.

We joined the school's teachers and students to have a get-together with the residents of the Anjing Senior Citizen's Home. We and the children put on a sign-language performance called "A Thankful Heart".

At the end of a busy day, we put the classroom desks together to serve as a makeshift bed; nevertheless, we all slept like logs.

This get-together was also fun for the students. Here they are having a great time.

Teachers of the school told us that the students had become much livelier and that there was a lot more laughter around after our arrival.

Just before our departure, the students scramble to write us farewell notes. Their letters were sincere and moved us deeply. All we wanted to say was: "Anjing, we'll see you next year!"

BEIJING DRIFTERS

The rootless or the free?

Piāoliú Qīngchūn

漂流青春

Article and Photographs by
Asen

XIONG RUI:
24-year-old radio DJ, Xiong Rui, comes from Hubei Province. Xiong worked in Shanghai prior to arriving in Beijing in 2008. One of SOHO's (Small Office/Home Office) many tenants, he works primarily from home.

The term "Beijing drifters" is used to refer to those who live and work in Beijing without a Beijing *hukou* (registered residency permit). It is an all-expansive term that applies to anyone from college graduates to people struggling just to get by. One could also interpret it as a reference to the phenomenon of increased migration that has occurred in China since the reform and opening up policies took hold.

Some say that being a "drifter" has a deeper meaning: a rootless and insecure soul who doesn't belong anywhere. Ask a drifter and you'll find otherwise, for behind these vagabonds usually lies a person who expects nothing and fears no one; a person who is free. Let's take a look at two Beijing drifters.

Xiong Rui's studio: a mixing console, computer, microphone and one giant desk. Everyday he downloads more than 400MB worth of material, comes up with his own skits, records his program, and sends it off to the radio station.

For breaks from the graveyard shift, he enjoys taking long walks down empty streets, stopping only for cigarettes along the way.

"I expect Beijing to be one of many stops in my life."

Perhaps the only one who shares Xiong's nocturnal sleeping schedule is his best buddy and companion, the quiet Mu Cun.

Waking up at 7:00 P.M. to greet a new day. Xiong's typical routine is "half up to my work and half up to me."

Xiong checks his mailbox regularly for postcards from friends. This is a vital link to an outside world made sparse by his hermitic lifestyle.

LI XIAN:
Hailing from Hunan, 25-year-old Li Xian is on the cusp of graduating with a degree in film.

Her thesis, job-hunting and internship have taken the forefront in her life. As a result, tidiness has been put on the backburner— much to the dismay of her three roommates.

Hukou or not, at the end of the day, she's still just another sleeping face on the train.

Li's short-term goals include a good job, nice apartment, and above all a completely independent lifestyle in the nation's capital.

Primping in the afternoon before going to her internship.

Sitting down for a taste of her hometown. Ordinarily Li Xian would feel embarrassed eating out in the open on campus, but with graduation on the horizon, it just doesn't seem to matter anymore.

Living a life on the run is much like crossing wide streets—it just doesn't feel safe somehow.

HUMAN
HUTONGS

Yǒu Yì Tiān,   Wǒmen Yě Jiāng Lǎo Qù
有一天，我们也将老去

By Asen
Photographs by Asen, Zhang Hengquan,
and X-Man Photography
Translated by Ginger Huang

Since modern China can be full of light, glitz and Western glam, we thought it would be a nice change to find the real roots of today's country. After scouring China with cameras and observation crews, what we were looking for sat peacefully on our own street corner. These characters are the gentle lotus that glide quietly with the water; they are the wind that elusively sways with the grass. They are the humilty of this country, found in every park, resting place and waning shadow. They are the origins of this country, the people who carry tradition on their backs, often unnoticed amidst the bustle, swerving traffic and today's fast-paced generations. They are China's human *hutongs*, strong in presence, but perhaps a big hidden in modernity.

A weathered musician performs for his young community.

Stretching and preparing for her morning walk, this rural lady wonders where the cameras come from.

A local granny in Anhui Province

A grandfather sits in front of his computer, curiously wandering through the new and vast world of the Internet.

A small square, frequented by the elderly in Yuanbei Community, mostly used for exercise.

Many of these children's photos have been sent from this lady's hometown in Jiangxi. There, when a child is born, it is tradition to show his/her photo to the elderly.

An elder in Yuanbei Community plays mahjong in the commons. By and by, the sun pales, and winter days are worn away.

Her son is busy with his career, only visiting his mother on important festivals and birthdays.

Jiang (right) and Wang (left) have two daughters, one in Beijing and one married in Japan. Their last family reunion was several years ago.

Li, 94. Having been committed to Songtang Hospital for nine years, she is the longest dweller here. On her walls hang gifts and pictures brought by volunteers.

Playing ball

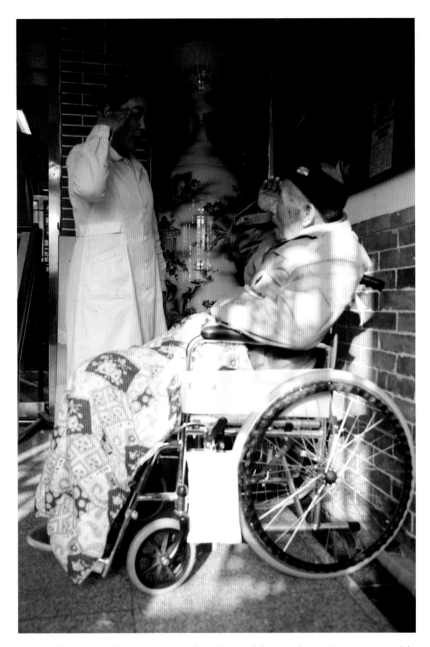

Jiang, 87. He usually greets people with a soldier's salute. He expresses his emotions this way, too.

Jiang enjoys listening to the fairy tales Nurse Dong reads to him.

It is getting chilly, but in warmer days, she rests in the gardens.

Jiang used to work for the government and can speak Japanese. Many of the patrons from that hospital had a past similar to his—all were good.

THE
RELIC
RESOUNDS

The Great Wall and the beauty that keeps
us coming back, century after century

Chángchéng de Huíxiǎng

长城的回响

Article and Photographs by
Josh Haller

Long heralded as China's most
recognizable cultural symbol, this
testament to fortitude, diligence and
social responsibility leaves little wonder as to
what it is that continues to draw travelers from
both abroad and at home to its storied towers
and the amazing perspectives it has to offer
of outer-Beijing's breathtaking landscapes. In
this Kaleidoscope, Josh Haller provides us with
a glimpse into the Wall's ace-in-the-hole: its
natural beauty, with photos that speak to the
admirer—whether seasoned or just-arrived—in
all of us.

The ancient crags of Tower 8 serve as a reminder of how far/high we've come.

Between the cracks of the First Tower of Chinese Civilization.

Contrary to popular belief, a day at the Wall is far from a walk in the park.

"There were 27 towers total. It took us about 6 hours to hike it. We hiked from Jinshanling (金山岭) to Simatai (司马台)."

A gateway into the past.

Looks (and distances) can be deceiving at such heights.

The modern world rears its head: Highway.

Into the white

Rustic renovations, with brown paint.

Slightly out of place (taken after Tower 20).

A room with a view (Tower 22).

A centuries-old occupation: repairing the Wall
(taken after Tower 23).

A look back at a day and a marvel.

LIVING AT THE FOOT OF THE QIN GREAT WALL

Qín Chángchéng • Rénjiā

秦长城·人家

By He Hongtao
Photographs by Liu Jianfeng, He Hongtao
Translated by Yang Yugong

The relatively better-preserved Hongbangou ruins of the Qin Great Wall

In August, 2008, led by Mr. Dong Yaohui, a well-known Great Wall expert, we, the reporters of *The World of Chinese*, took a hiking tour surveying the ruins of the Qin Great Wall located in Guyang County, Baotou City of the Inner Mongolia Autonomous Region. During the tour, we saw a different part of the Great Wall.

Guyang County lies in the Western part of the Daqing Mountain range of the Inner Mongolia Plateau. Mountains and hills account for 90% of the county's total area. Guyang is especially famous for its ruins of the Qin Great Wall, the best protected section from the Qin Dynasty (BC221-BC206). The section extends 85 kilometers along the rise and fall of the Yinshan Mountain range, which offers a spectacular landscape alongside its long history. However, many sections of the ruins have been severely damaged due to geological changes, weather erosion and farmland encroachment. In some areas the ruins are hardly recognizable.

The weather-beaten ruins of the Beacon Fire Site

The barely recognizable remains of the Qin Great Wall

Guyang is a little town with a small population. Strolling along the streets, you often see elderly people chatting at the doors of their houses and children playing by the roadside. Local people told us that many young people have gone to work in the big cities such as Baotou or Huhhot, and they only come back once a year during the Spring Festival.

Town people chatting on the street

Children of the vegetable sellers

A grain porte

Walking along the Qin Great Wall, we met many kind-hearted local residents and we were deeply impressed by their sincerity and simplicity.

When we were not sure in what direction we were heading, Mr. Gao Maolin, one of the villagers, kindly showed us the way. He was a motorcyclist roaming freely through the mountains.

On the road we sometimes saw shepherds. This man in the picture lives in Chenjiacun Village; he herds more than 30 sheep every day from ten o'clock in the morning till six in the evening. Normally, he has only two meals every day. He told us there had been 50 or 60 households in Chenjiacun Village. However, in recent years, more and more young people left home to work in the cities. Many families have moved to Guyang or Baotou. Now only a dozen households remain in the village.

Youmian, a kind of oat-made food, is a local specialty. Customarily, the hospitable people of Guyang entertain their guests from afar by serving them this food with a delicious stock made with fresh mushrooms and mutton. Once when we stopped by a farm house, the hostess Ms. Zhao Yu'e cooked the authentic youmian noodles for us.

The residents along the Great Wall build their houses conforming to the local geography with native materials. A farm house on the mountain under the blue sky combined with golden sunflowers is a beautiful picture.

With mutual trust, local residents seldom lock their doors; they simply tie them with string.

There are no places of entertainment in the village. Most of the time, this boy and girl play right outside their house. The sister loves to sing local folk songs, while the little boy prefers to play with his toy excavator.

The houses are built with mud, which erodes with time and rain. The villagers have to repair their houses once in a while.

More and more children in the village have gone to city schools with their parents. This girl who goes to the local school has fewer friends, so she always spends the vacations with her pet dog "Doudou".

The greatest wish of most parents in Guyang is for their children to leave this mountainous area for college. The little girl in this picture is 6-year-old Cairong. She lives in Xiaowutu Village of Yinhao Town; she loves school. In order to have a better learning environment, her father brought her to Baotou with him where she started kindergarten. He works hard in the city to make money for her education. It has been a big challenge for him, but as a father, he thinks it worthwhile.

图书在版编目(CIP)数据

镜像中国＝China in Scope/《汉语世界》杂志社编. —
北京:商务印书馆,2011
ISBN 978 - 7 - 100 - 07402 - 5

Ⅰ.①镜…　Ⅱ.①汉…　Ⅲ.①中国—概况—画册
Ⅳ.①K92-64

中国版本图书馆 CIP 数据核字(2010)第 191318 号

镜像中国

《汉语世界》杂志社　编

商 务 印 书 馆 出 版
(北京王府井大街36号　邮政编码 100710)
商 务 印 书 馆 发 行
北京瑞古冠中印刷厂印刷
ISBN 978 - 7 - 100 - 07402 - 5

2011 年 4 月第 1 版　　开本 889×1194　1/16
2011 年 4 月北京第 1 次印刷　印张 7¼
定价:89.00 元